I LOVE BIRTHDAY PARTIES

Which one would you choose?

By

Hannele Rämö

Hello!
My name is Esther and I **LOVE** parties!
Today is my friend Anna's birthday party.
Yesterday we went to a store to buy a present for her.
I wanted to choose the best gift for Anna. It was difficult to choose. Eventually mom said that we have to go and I had to decide.
I took a monkey who laughs when you squeeze its hand. I have played with one like this at my friend's house.
I think it was so funny! I can't wait to give the present.

The shop was full of lovely toys.
It took
a long
long
time
to think what to buy.

I LOVE to wear fancy clothes. I could wear my dresses every day!
I don't know what the best dress today would be.
I'll try them all!
Hmmm...
Which one would you pick?

Now I have to decide what to wear for the party. I love dresses. I have many lovely dresses.

CLOTHES
I'll take this one with roses.
It's so pretty!
I haven't used it for a while.
What a mess!
But now I have to hurry. Arranging can wait.

My sister makes **wonderful** hairdos. She promised to do my hair today. I can choose which hairdo I want today.

No...too ordinary....

No....I just used this headband....

No...It's too fluffy...

I want this! It's so lovely!

Next I need stockings and shoes.
I have
such lovely stockings and shoes.

Actually I don't like stockings. They keep itching me. But I will wear
one pair at the party. Which one would you pick?

I'll take these pony stockings.
I love ponies.''

Which shoes
would I wear?

Finally I am Ready! I have to hurry. Mom is waiting for me.

OH NO!
HELP!

Stupid stairs! My knee is hurting!

OH no! My knee is bleeding and it hurts very much!
MOM!!!
My skirt is dirty and my stockings are torn.
MOM!!!

Mom cleans the wound and finds the plasters. Luckily mom
has bought lots of different kinds of plasters.
Mommy said that we need them very often.
All the plasters are

SO LOVELY!

I can chooce whatever plaster I want. They are all so nice!
Which one would you pick?

I think I need two. Just in case.

Now I have to change my clothes. A new dress and new
stockings. Finally ready!
Oh... I also want this unicorn headband.
Now I have to run.

No, I think maybe I should walk....

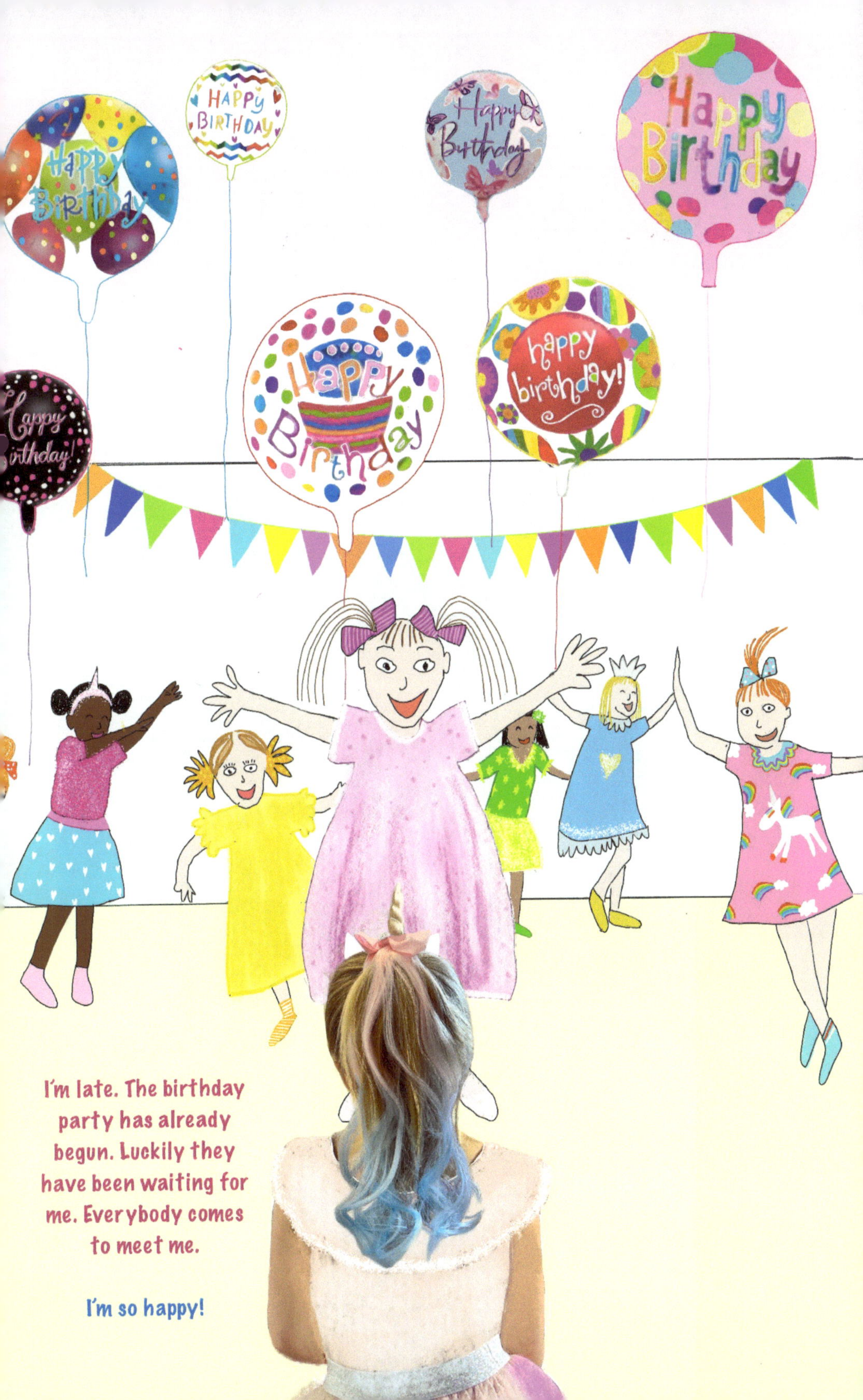
I'm late. The birthday party has already begun. Luckily they have been waiting for me. Everybody comes to meet me.

I'm so happy!

Actually I don't like stockings. They keep itching me. But I will wear
one pair at the party. Which one would you pick?

I'll take these pony stockings.
I love ponies."

We are playing bottlerolling and Anna opens the present
which the bottle points at.
She gets
LOVELY
presents.
She also likes my gift.

Create your Unicorn
What is the
the
best gift?
I think
the best gift is that you
came here to celebrate
with me!
Without you there wouldn't
be a party!

HAPPY
BIRTHDAY
Anna said she
got the most
beautiful
birthday cards.

Let's go and eat delicacies!
I LOVE
cakes and candy and muffins and lemonade!
Birthday parties are the best!

Anna had a surprise for us. We got to chooce ice
cream from Anna's self made ice cream bar.
It was AWESOME !
Can you quess which one I chose?